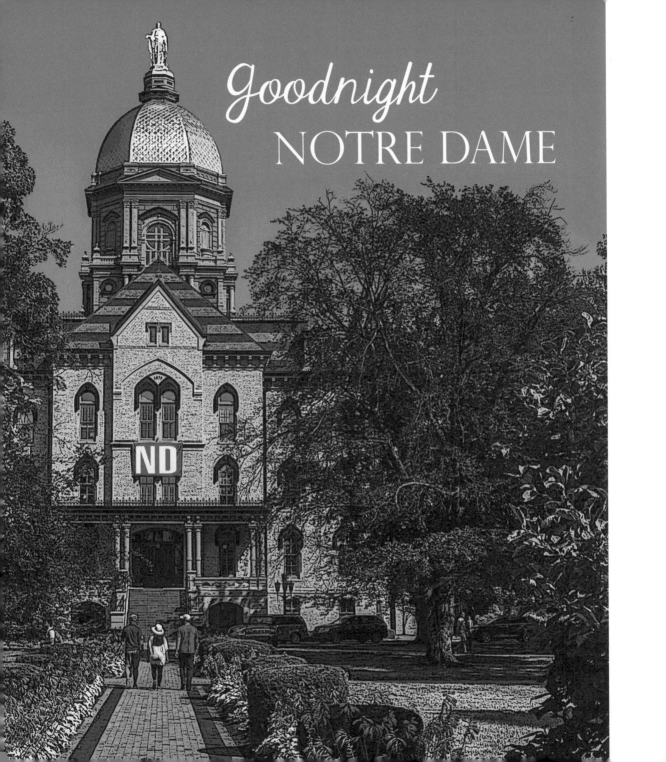

Goodnight
NOTRE DAME

Just north of South Bend, IN
is the place that she calls home.
Inside, are her legends, traditions
and a giant golden dome.

Fair Catch Corby, First down Moses
and Touchdown Jesus guide the light,
as the sun sets on each Irish night.

Goodnight Mr. Notre Dame.
Goodnight to the Gipper,
the legendary runner, passer and kicker.

Goodnight to the Basilica
and her bells that ring.

Goodnight Mother Mary

whose praises we sing.

Goodnight to the Grotto
and the prayers lifted high.

Goodnight to Rockne's house
and the fans victory cry.

Goodnight Gold, Goodnight Blue
Goodnight to her traditions, old and new.

Goodnight to the Leprechaun
with his dukes held high,

And bless the Irish Guard as we watch them dance by.

Goodnight to the Four Horsemen

and the victories they led.

Goodnight to the President
they called Father Ted.

Goodnight to the birds
who rest on her lake,

Goodnight to her visitors
and the memories they make.

Goodnight to the log cabin
where it all began,

Goodnight to the fighting Irish
in all the lands.

Goodnight God, Country and Notre Dame.
Goodnight to all the echoes calling her name.

Jennifer Bethell

True love for Notre Dame was instilled in us at a very young age, but it wasn't until I was older that I fully understand what this University meant to our family. As a small child I can remember hearing stories about a good friend Moose, a golf game with Lou, and how my dad and his brothers would sell programs at the games when they were young. When I was old enough to understand what these stories meant, I realized Notre Dame was a part of me.

I hope to instill the same love of the Irish to my children and their children. My hope is that saying goodnight to the Basilica every night will remind them of where their parents married, saying goodnight to the cabin will remind my daughter where she was baptized, or to the stadium where our family has shared the experience of countless football games. Everyone has memories that keep their love of Notre Dame alive; I hope this book helps remind you and your family of that love.

Trevor Ruszkowski

Growing Up Irish seems to be a real thing in our families. As games were seen live as well as on the tv, it was always a part of our lives. We would walk across campus and it would not be strange to see Ara, Lou, Digger, Moose, or Father Ted.
Today with my family I make it a point to go to ND sporting events. Notre Dame is a magical place, where Blue and Gold seep into veins and I want that for my family and my parents wanted that for me. I have walked campus, sat and watched countless sporting events, and photographed some great sporting events as well. I wanted to take a tour of Notre Dame, then create some magic of my own by creating art out of the photos I took, so people will remember the campus, how they want to.

Goodnight
NOTRE DAME

CPSIA information can be obtained
at www.ICGtesting.com
Printed in the USA
LVHW071352221021
701202LV00007B/56